My Very First Story Time

Goldilocks
and the Three Bears

Retold by Ronne Randall
Illustrated by Tim Budgen

cottage

Daddy Bear

Mummy Bear

Baby Bear

big bed

tiny bed

middle-sized
bed

Daddy Bear's
porridge

Baby Bear's
porridge

Mummy Bear's
porridge

big chair

tiny chair

middle-sized chair

ONCE UPON A TIME, there were three bears. Great big Daddy Bear, middle-sized Mummy Bear, and teeny-tiny Baby Bear. They always had porridge for breakfast.

One morning, their porridge was much too hot, so
the three bears went out for a walk while it cooled down.

A little girl called Goldilocks was walking through the woods, too. When she came to the three bears' cottage, she peeped in through the open window.

"Mmm!" she said. "Porridge. It smells so
yummy. It will fill my hungry tummy!"
In through the window she climbed.

Goldilocks tasted Daddy Bear's porridge. "Yuk!" she said. "Too salty!"

Next, she tried Mummy Bear's porridge. "Yuk!" she said. "Too sweet!"

Last of all, she tried Baby Bear's porridge. "Mmm!" she said. "Just right!" She ate it all up, right to the very last drop.

Goldilocks tiptoed further into the cottage and spied three chairs. "I think I'll sit down," she said.

The great big chair was
so hard she jumped
straight off.

The middle-sized chair
was so soft she got stuck.

The teeny-tiny chair looked just
right. But when Goldilocks sat
on it, CRACK! It fell to pieces.

Goldilocks was feeling more and more curious, so up the stairs she went. There were three beds, and she tried them all. The great big bed was too high.

The middle-sized bed was too low.

But the teeny-tiny bed felt just right.
Goldilocks lay down and fell
fast asleep.

Soon, the three bears came home for their breakfast.

"Someone's been eating my porridge!" growled Daddy Bear.

"And someone's been eating my porridge!" said Mummy Bear.

"Someone's been eating my porridge and has eaten up every last drop!" cried Baby Bear.

The three bears looked at their chairs.
"Someone's been sitting in my chair!"
growled Daddy Bear.

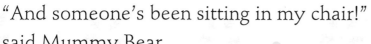
"And someone's been sitting in my chair!"
said Mummy Bear.

"Someone's been sitting in my chair and has
broken it all to pieces!" cried Baby Bear.

The three bears marched upstairs.
"Someone's been sleeping in my bed!"
growled Daddy Bear.

"And someone's
been sleeping in
my bed!" said
Mummy Bear.

"Someone's been sleeping in my bed and she's still here!" cried Baby Bear.

All the noise woke Goldilocks. What a fright she had when she saw the three bears standing over her!

"Oh!" she cried.
"Oh! Oh! Oh!"

Goldilocks jumped up, scampered downstairs, and went as fast as she could out of the three bears' house. She never went back again.

And the three bears never again left their window open when they went for a walk in the woods.

Point to the teeny-tiny bear.

Point to the middle-sized chair.

Point to the biggest bowl.

Which bear will go to sleep in which bed?

Find the shortest way for
Goldilocks to get back home.